Miss Renée's Mice Go to an Exhibition

By Elizabeth Stokes Hoffman

Illustrated by Dawn Peterson

Down East Books
Camden, Maine

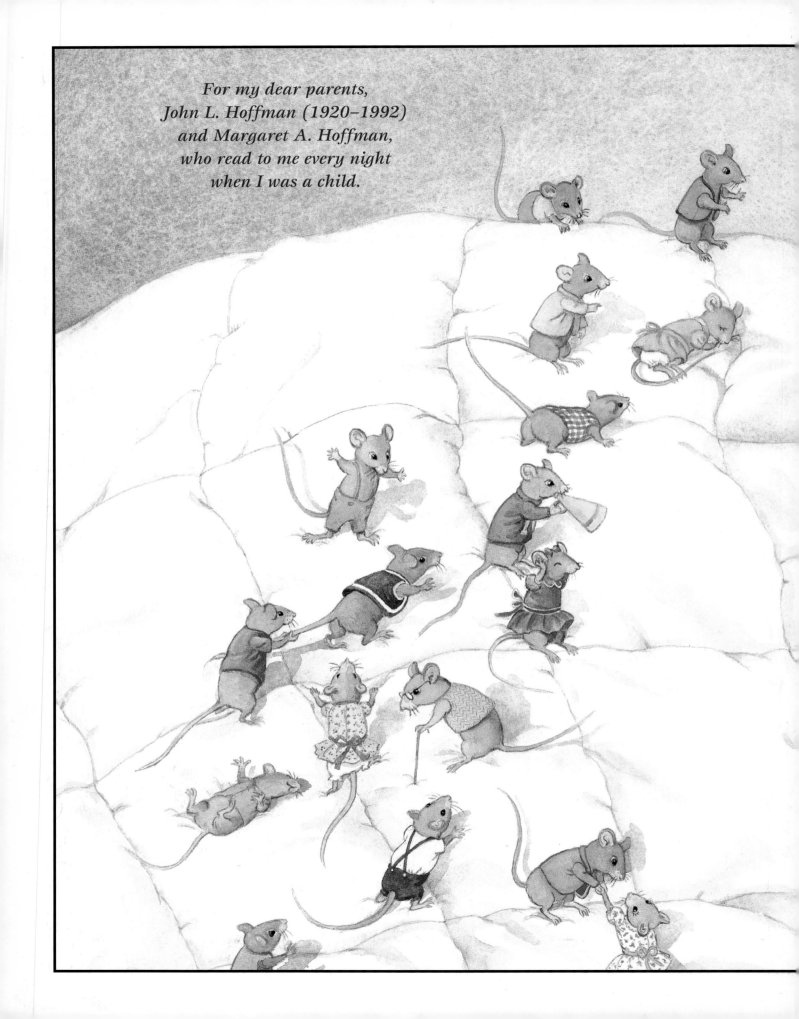

For my dear parents,
John L. Hoffman (1920–1992)
and Margaret A. Hoffman,
who read to me every night
when I was a child.

Early morning was not Miss Renée's favorite time of day, and she liked it even less when dozens of mice were squeaking in her ear.

"Please?" they cried. "Ple-e-e-ase take us to the exhibition?"

Miss Renée was a miniature maker. Today she was going to an important exhibition where she would have a whole table to show off her dollhouses full of tiny furniture and other beautiful things that she made by hand.

"You know perfectly well I can't take you," said Miss Renée. "Real mice would frighten people."

"Would not!" squeaked the mice.

"Would so," said Miss Renée. "Even sensible people can be scared of mice, and if people are scared, they won't buy any of my little tables or chairs or rugs, and then I won't have enough money to repair the chimney, and next winter we'll all freeze. Now pipe down and eat your breakfast."

But the mice wouldn't pipe down.

They began marching in a circle on the kitchen table, banging their spoons and cups. "Unfair to mice! Unfair to mice!" they squeaked.

The banging and squeaking grew louder and louder. "UNFAIR TO MICE! UNFAIR TO MICE!! *UNFAIR TO MICE!!!*"

Miss Renée stuck her fingers in her ears. The trouble was, it *was* unfair. Ever since the mice had moved in with her, they had made themselves very handy around the house. They had even helped build some of the furniture she was taking to the exhibition.

But what on earth could she do?

Suddenly a bright idea popped into her head.

"All right, you mice!" she said. "Stop that racket and listen to me. If I take you to the exhibition, can you sit *perfectly still* and be *perfectly quiet* and pretend that you are toy mice?"

"Yes! Yes!" squealed the mice, jumping with joy. "Perfectly still! Perfectly quiet!"

Miss Renée loaded up her car, and away they drove, down a long, winding dirt road and onto a big highway and all the way into the city of Portland.

The exhibition was in the ballroom of a fancy hotel.

Miss Renée waved hello to the other miniature makers. Then she unpacked her dollhouses and furniture and all her other beautiful little things and arranged them on the table.

The mice hopped out of her pockets, where they had been hiding, and sat down on the tiny chairs and sofas and climbed into the beds.

"Now, remember," whispered Miss Renée, winking at them, "not one peep! You're toy mice."

The mice winked back. They stuck their arms and legs out stiff. They stared straight ahead with glassy eyes. They looked exactly like toy mice.

Crowds of people began filing into the hotel. They had come from near and far to see the miniatures. Some of them, especially the ones from away, looked very wealthy.

Through the window Miss Renée spied a white-haired lady in a purple velvet hat and silver shoes stepping out of a limousine. "I bet that one's got heaps of money!" said Miss Renée. "I hope she spends it all at my table."

The ballroom was a wonderland of miniatures. People wandered up and down saying "Ooh" and "Ahh" at the rooms furnished in every style, at the sparkling chandeliers and perfect little dinner tables set with shiny silverware and make-believe food, at the tiny beds covered with patchwork quilts and piled high with pillows.

Around every corner there was something new to look at: bathtubs and sinks and iceboxes, potted plants and chessboards and musical instruments, bicycles and newspapers and umbrella stands and wheelbarrows and shrubbery.

Of course there were dolls, too—cloth ones and wooden ones and old-fashioned china ones—but none of them were nearly as interesting as Miss Renée's mice.

"Oh, how adorable!" everyone exclaimed. "Why, they look just like real mice! How much are they? I'd like to buy one, please."

Miss Renée smiled and said, "I'm sorry, my mice aren't for sale. But everything else is."

Miss Renée felt very proud that her clever idea was working so well.

The mice were proud, too. They puffed themselves up and stuck their arms and legs out even straighter.

But after hearing hundreds and hundreds of people say, "Oh, how precious! Oh, what cute little toy mice!" Miss Renée didn't feel quite as happy. Everyone was so busy admiring her mice that they didn't even notice her beautiful furniture.

The mice, on the other hand, just felt happier and happier.

Miss Renée gave them a sour look.

By lunchtime Miss Renée had sold nothing but a footstool and was feeling very peevish. She had practically forgotten that it was her idea for the mice to pretend to be toys. She took a great big peanut butter sandwich out of her pocketbook and began to eat it all by herself.

The mice sniffed the air hungrily. "Where's our lunch?" they whispered.

"Oh, you don't get any," said Miss Renée. "Toy mice don't need lunch."

The mice began to whimper. They had been too excited to finish their breakfast, and now their stomachs were rumbling. Sitting perfectly still for hours was hard work.

"YUM!" said Miss Renée, taking another big bite of sandwich. In her heart she knew she was being mean, but she couldn't help it. While the poor mice squirmed in their seats, she ate up the rest of the sandwich and smacked her lips.

At that very moment, a waiter on his way to the hotel dining room walked through the ballroom carrying an enormous silver tray piled high with exquisite desserts.

The aroma of chocolate and vanilla and cinnamon and fruit and nuts and flaky pastry filled the dollhouses and made the mice's noses twitch until they couldn't stand it for another second.

They leaped off their chairs and sofas and out of their beds and swarmed out of the dollhouses and up the waiter's trouser legs.

"*EEEEEEYYYAAAAIII!!!!*" screamed the waiter, flinging his tray

in the air. Cakes and cookies and pies and little dishes of pudding flew everywhere. A coconut macaroon hit Miss Renée on the nose. Everyone began screaming, "MICE! MICE! REAL MICE!"

Some of the people ran out of the ballroom as fast as they could. Others leaped up onto the tables or climbed the drapery to escape the mice. It was pandemonium!

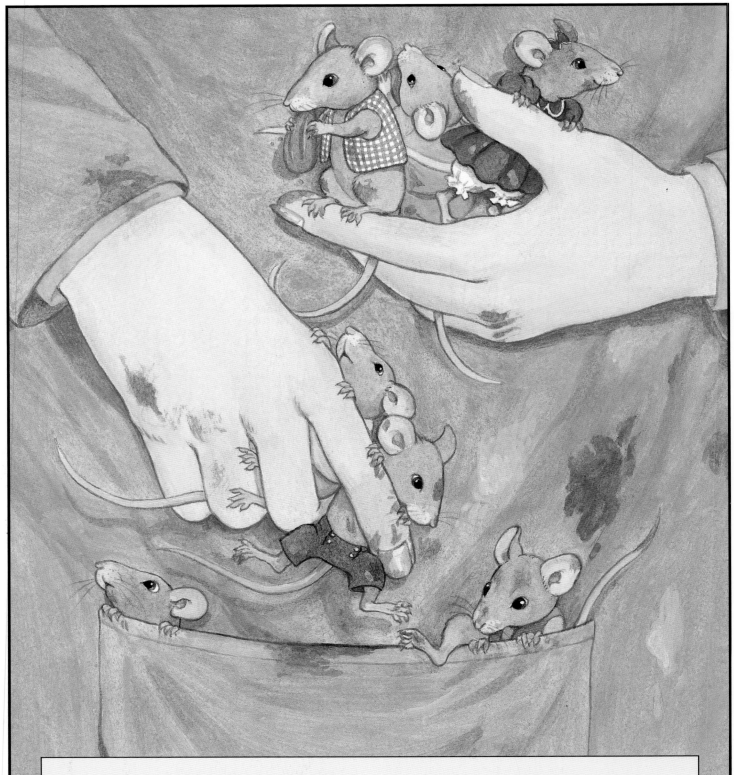

"Oh, for heaven's sake," muttered Miss Renée. "They're just little mice. They're not monsters." She plucked her mice out of the sticky dessert mess and dropped them back into her pockets.

When the uproar died down, everybody climbed off the tables and down from the drapery. They stood in a circle around Miss Renée, glaring at her. The hotel manager began to yell.

Just when Miss Renée was thinking things couldn't get much worse, the elegant lady in the purple velvet hat came *click-click-click*ing up in her silver shoes. She pointed her finger at Miss Renée and said, "You! You are zee vun who bringed live mouses!"

Miss Renée, who was covered with cookie crumbs and chocolate and dabs of pie filling, felt very shabby and ashamed of herself. "I'm afraid so," she mumbled.

The lady in the purple hat beamed so that her whole face lit up. "I LOVE MOUSES!" she said. "I come from my country all zee vay to Maine because I hear it is famous for mouses, but instead I find out it is famous for mooses. Mooses is very majestic, but zey do not fit in my pockets."

Dozens of mice popped out of her pockets and waved hello to Miss Renée's mice.

"My, vat beautiful little furnitures you make!" said the purple hat lady. "I vill buy zem all, please."

When the exhibition was over, Miss Renée and the purple hat lady and both groups of mice went to the hotel dining room for tea, and everybody had a wonderful time.

Except, of course, for the waiter.

Story copyright © 2003 by Elizabeth Stokes Hoffman
Illustrations copyright © 2003 by Dawn Peterson
ISBN 0-89272-581-8
Printed in China / RPS

2   4   5   3   1

Down East Books
P.O. Box 679, Camden, ME 04843
Book orders: 1-800-766-1670
www.downeastbooks.com